For Katherine, Harvey & Maud – Z.S. & N.L.

For my mum, Angela. And my weirdo, Joel. – M.F.

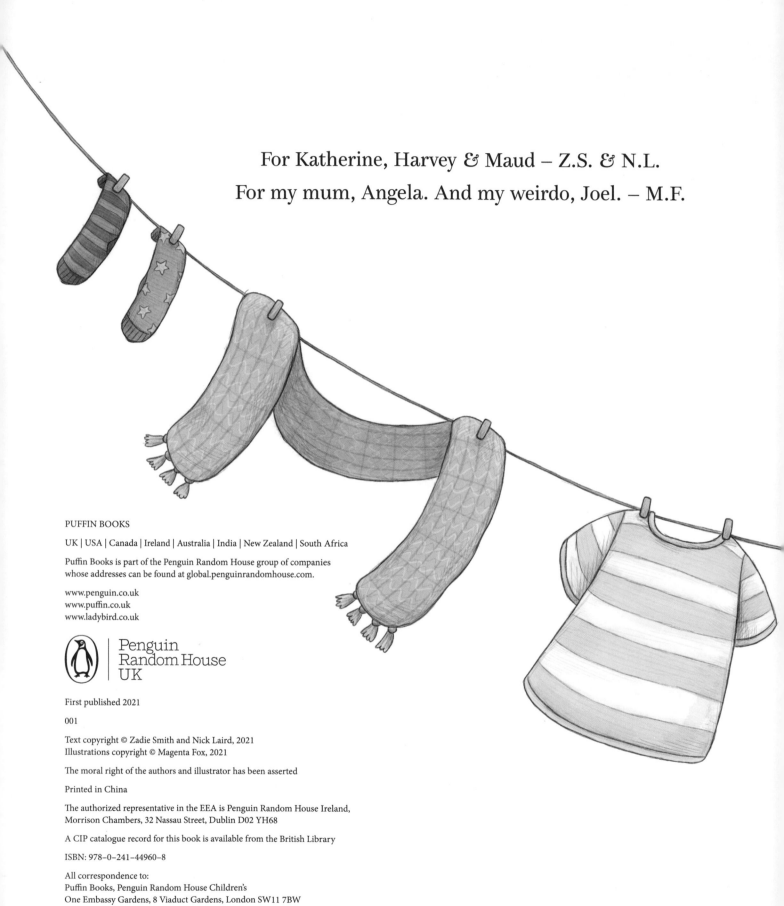

PUFFIN BOOKS

UK | USA | Canada | Ireland | Australia | India | New Zealand | South Africa

Puffin Books is part of the Penguin Random House group of companies
whose addresses can be found at global.penguinrandomhouse.com.

www.penguin.co.uk
www.puffin.co.uk
www.ladybird.co.uk

Penguin
Random House
UK

First published 2021

001

Text copyright © Zadie Smith and Nick Laird, 2021
Illustrations copyright © Magenta Fox, 2021

The moral right of the authors and illustrator has been asserted

Printed in China

The authorized representative in the EEA is Penguin Random House Ireland,
Morrison Chambers, 32 Nassau Street, Dublin D02 YH68

A CIP catalogue record for this book is available from the British Library

ISBN: 978–0–241–44960–8

All correspondence to:
Puffin Books, Penguin Random House Children's
One Embassy Gardens, 8 Viaduct Gardens, London SW11 7BW

FSC
www.fsc.org
MIX
Paper from
responsible sources
FSC® C018179

ZADIE SMITH   NICK LAIRD

WEIRDO

illustrated by
MAGENTA FOX

PUFFIN

It was Kit's birthday.

Her present was a soft, small, sleepy surprise.

She's perfect! Kit whispered.
But why's she dressed like that?

No-one knew.
The Surprise wasn't telling.

Kit left for school. The Surprise woke up.

She was surrounded.

But what is it?
chirped Derrick.
She clearly can't fly.

Not a cat. Too round,
said Dora.

Or a pug, Bob decided.
Those legs!

She don't do much, noted Derrick.
Actually, whispered the Surprise,
            I'm quite into Judo.

What's that now? barked Bob.
He was a bit deaf.

She just said she's a weirdo, sniggered Dora.

Are you a weirdo? asked Bob.
The Surprise didn't know what to say.

Oh, she's definitely a weirdo,
said Dora. *If you're not a cat
or a dog or a bird, you're a weirdo.*

According to the schedule, Bob announced,
it is now time to watch **Animal World**.
Do you watch **Animal World**? It's on the schedule.

I've only seen the judo,
whispered the Surprise.

TODAY is: Monday
7ᴬᴹ breakfast
8ᴬᴹ Animal World
9ᴬᴹ Animal World
10ᴬᴹ Animal World

She said she's always been a weirdo! shouted Dora, and with that,
Dora and Bob padded into the living room to watch telly,
with Derrick fluttering after.

The Surprise was left alone.

She thought about ways to make herself more like the others.

She sat down and felt sad.

Then she had an idea.

SURPRISE!

shouted the Surprise,
I can fly.

But just then,
a gust of wind came in
one window . . .

. . . and blew the Surprise out the other.

Oops,
she thought.

The Surprise was worried. Maybe she was going to
go into the clouds. Or up into forever overhead.

But just as she was floating past the last balcony,
when all seemed lost . . .

. . . She met somebody.

Hello, said the somebody, *I'm Emily Brookstein.*
And what's your name?
Everyone calls me Weirdo, said the Surprise.

Oh, they call me weirdo, too, said Emily Brookstein.
Life's too short not to be a weirdo.
Why do they think you're weird?

I think, said the Surprise,
because I am unaware of the schedule.

Heaven save us from schedules! cried Emily,
and brought out a plate of coconut macaroons.

Now what's your real name?

I don't know. I'm Kit's
birthday present.

Are you indeed!
Well, I had an Aunt Melody
who looked a bit like you.
She was a weirdo.
Kept boiled eggs in her pocket
and stayed out dancing ever so late.

Oh.

The Surprise and Emily Brookstein
played cards,

and ate macaroons,

until the grandfather clock
struck three.

Emily said:
*I wish you could stay all day
but it must be about time
to take you back. Your Kit
will be getting home soon.*

When Kit saw the Surprise she gave her
a very long and very nice hug.

And the Surprise thought,
        Oh that's what I do. I get hugged.

You guys . . . said Kit. Meet Maud.

Maud, is it? murmured Bob,
who could hear perfectly
well when he wanted to.

*We were only a bit mean because we were
worried you might be a weirdo,*
said Dora.

Maud smiled and thought of Emily.
*I **am** a weirdo*, she said. *But I am also a Maud.*

Sorry about earlier, said Derrick.
Can you by any chance teach us some judo?

So they added judo to the schedule.